The *Answer*

Britt Wolfe

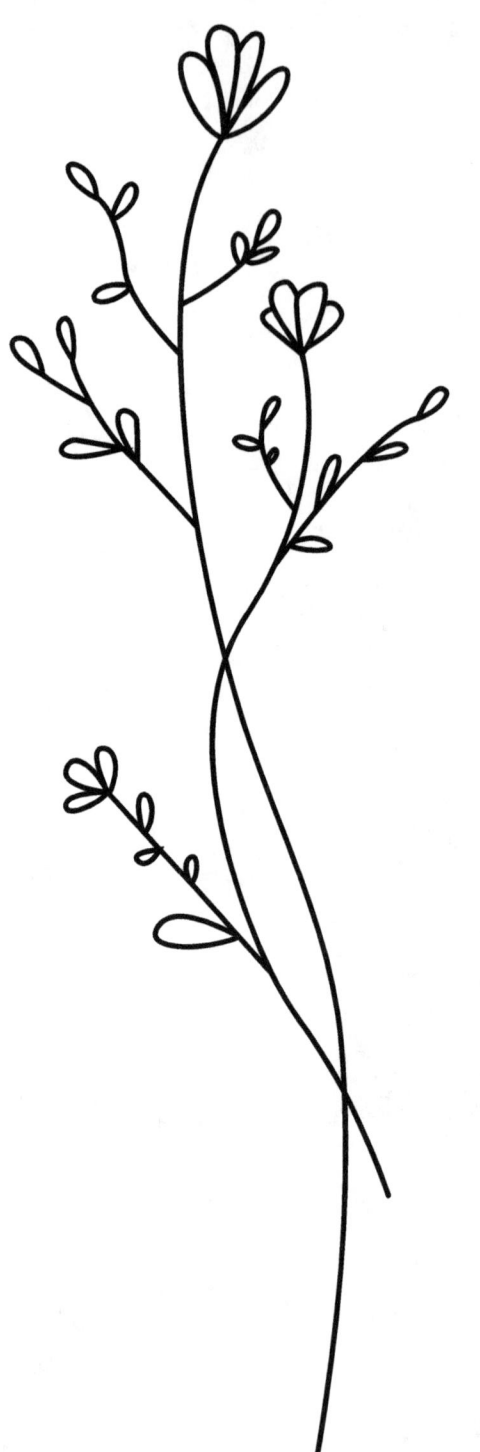

This Novella Is Dedicated to:

All The women who have faced heartbreak and doubt, who have wrestled with invisible and unimaginable choices – and who have chosen themselves, over and over again.

This is for the ones who walked away when staying seemed easier, who found courage in the quiet spaces, and who rose from the storms they thought would break them.

It is also for the women who have not yet found the strength to walk away, who are still searching for the light in the darkness, and who carry the weight of their stories quietly, day by day.

May you know your worth, your resilience, and your boundless capacity for better. May this story remind you that you are never alone, that your voice matters, and that choosing yourself is not just an act of bravery – it's a testament to your infinite strength.

The Answer
Is Inspired by: *Champagne Problems*
by Taylor Swift

When I first heard *Champagne Problems*, it struck me as more than just a heartbreak anthem—it felt like an unraveling of everything we hide behind polished smiles and perfect facades. It's a song about moments that seem simple from the outside but are filled with agony, strength, and truths too heavy to share. It's about the courage it takes to say 'no' when everyone expects you to say 'yes', and the heartbreak of walking away from something that the world believes is perfect but that you know in your heart isn't meant for you.

This story, inspired by Taylor Swift's extraordinary words, is my reflection on that bravery—on the strength it takes to reject a love that is bruised by control and abuse. It's about the invisible scars that others fail to see and the crushing loneliness that often follows choosing yourself. At its heart, it's a story about resilience, about reclaiming your voice when it feels like no one else is listening, and about surviving the storm of judgment to step into the light of freedom.

I hope this story resonates with you the way *Champagne Problems* has always spoken to me—a hauntingly beautiful reminder of the courage it takes to choose your own path, no matter how difficult it may be.

Peace, Love, and Inspiration,

Britt Wolfe

The Proposal

The weight of four years—long nights of study sessions, mounting pressure, and the silent sacrifices her family had made—finally lifted as Cara placed the last period on her final exam. It wasn't an extravagant finish, nor did it feel like some kind of Hollywood montage where her future suddenly crystallized. It was quieter than that, simpler. Just relief.

She had walked out of the exam hall with a lightness she hadn't known in years, her steps unsteady with the kind of exhaustion that only came from giving everything to something you weren't even sure was yours to begin with. Political science had always been Jasper's suggestion—well, insistence, really. "You've got the brain for it," he'd told her more times than she could count. And when Cara didn't have the heart to argue, she let him steer her toward it, the way he steered her toward so much in her life.

Now, that chapter was closed. And here she was, swept into a glittering whirlwind of silk gowns and polished suits at one of Lehigh University's senior year galas. The gymnasium-turned-ballroom was barely recognizable, transformed with strings of lights that hung like stars and tables draped in gold and white linen. The scent of fresh roses mingled with the faint tang of champagne, and every corner hummed with the kind of energy that only came from young people on the brink of their futures. Everyone looked effortless. Everything looked perfect.

Except Cara didn't feel effortless or perfect. Not tonight. Not for a long time.

"Smile," Jasper whispered as his hand slid possessively to her lower back. "You'll want to remember this night."

Cara forced her lips to curve upward, tilting her head just enough to look adoring but not too much to invite questions. This was what everyone expected of them: the golden couple. He in his perfectly tailored tuxedo that matched his sharp, clean features; she in a gown she'd chosen only because Jasper said it "brought out her eyes." From the outside, they were flawless, enviable even. Their friends thought she was the luckiest girl alive. People stopped her at the coffee shops on campus to tell her so.

Her parents—proud and a little starstruck by Jasper's wealthy family—had said it often enough to make her nauseous.

Lucky. Lucky, lucky, lucky. The word clung to her like perfume she could never wash off, its sweetness turning acrid the longer she wore it.

The band switched to a slower song, and Jasper tugged her closer, his lips brushing her ear. "Let's go," he said, his voice low and coaxing, but not without the steel beneath it that made her stomach tighten.

"I want to stay," she replied, keeping her voice calm, steady. Her gaze swept the room, lingering on the table where her classmates sat, laughing and toasting their glasses. This was the end of something. It felt like a moment worth lingering in.

Jasper's hand stilled on her waist. He tilted his head, his expression neutral, but Cara felt the shift immediately. "I think we've stayed long enough," he said, each word deliberate, measured.

She stepped back slightly, her brows drawing together. "You don't have to stay if you don't want to. I'll get a ride home." It wasn't defiance—it was careful, calculated compromise, the kind she had learned to offer him in their four years together.

But compromise didn't sit well with Jasper. His jaw tightened, his smile unwavering as he glanced around the room, aware of the eyes that might be on them. "Cara," he said softly, but with a weight that made her pulse quicken. "Don't be difficult."

"I'm not being difficult," she replied, keeping her voice light. "I just want one more dance."

For a moment, Jasper didn't move. Then he let out a soft laugh, the kind that sounded charming to anyone who didn't know better. "Alright," he said, releasing her waist. "One more dance."

Cara exhaled, relieved, but that relief was short-lived. Jasper stepped away, walking toward the edge of the room. The message was clear: she could have her dance, but she wouldn't have it with him.

Her cheeks burned, but she turned back toward the dance floor, pretending not to notice the curious looks from the nearby tables. It didn't matter. She wouldn't let it matter. She moved to the music with her classmates, letting herself smile as the tension in her chest began to loosen.

But the reprieve didn't last long. Jasper was beside her again, his hand on her elbow, his grip just a little too firm. "We're leaving," he said, his tone leaving no room for discussion.

She wanted to argue, to say that she wasn't ready, that this was her night too. But the edge in his voice froze her, and the small knot of rebellion that had taken root in her stomach unraveled. "Fine," she said quietly, letting him lead her toward the exit.

The air outside was cool and sharp, a stark contrast to the warmth of the ballroom. Jasper didn't speak as he guided her to his car, his jaw tight and his movements clipped. Cara's own nerves felt raw and exposed, the silence between them stretching taut as they drove back to her dorm. She glanced at him once or twice, but his expression didn't soften.

When they reached her dorm's parking lot, Jasper seemed to shake off whatever storm had been brewing inside him. He smiled as he retrieved the bottle of Dom Pérignon from the back seat, his mood suddenly light and playful. "To us," he said as he popped the cork, the champagne fizzing over the rim of the bottle.

"To us," she repeated, though the words felt hollow.

Jasper tilted the bottle, letting the champagne fizz over the rim as he chuckled softly. He glanced at her, his charm dialled up, though his earlier coldness still clung to the air between them. "Come on," he said, stepping out of the car with the bottle in hand. The cool night air hit her as he opened her door, holding out a hand. "Let's celebrate properly."

Cara hesitated, but her body moved on autopilot, taking his hand as she stepped onto the curb. The dorm loomed ahead, its harsh fluorescent lights stark against the darkness. Jasper led the way, his grip firm but not painful, his pace brisk as though he'd already made up his mind about how the night would go. Cara glanced at the bottle of Dom Pérignon in his other hand, its gold label shimmering in the dim light. It felt out of place here, too lavish, too perfect for the scuffed concrete steps and linoleum hallways of student housing.

As they climbed the stairs to her private room, the echo of their footsteps filled the space. Cara couldn't help but notice the silence that stretched between them, heavy and unyielding. Her private room—an arrangement that Jasper had insisted on and helped pay for—felt impossibly far away with every step. It wasn't just the physical distance; it was the weight of knowing she had let him have this kind of power over her life.

He stopped at her door, pulling her key from his pocket like it belonged to him, like she belonged to him. The gesture, once something she might have found thoughtful, now felt stifling. He pushed the door open, and she followed, her gaze lingering on the familiar space. The neatly made bed, the curated bookshelf, the framed photos of her family—it all felt smaller now, as though the walls had shifted closer together.

Jasper set the champagne bottle on her desk with deliberate care, then turned back to her, his expression softening into something that looked like affection. "Wait here," he said, his voice low but firm. He crossed the room, flicking on the bedside lamp, its warm glow casting long shadows across the walls. The tension in Cara's chest grew heavier with each second that passed, her pulse quickening as he turned back toward her, his hand slipping into the jacket pocket of his tux.

And then, before she could even process the shift, Jasper knelt in front of her, pulling a velvet box from his pocket. The world seemed to tilt as he opened it, the diamond inside sparkling like something out of a dream.

"Cara," Jasper said, his voice warm and sure. "I want you to be my forever."

Her heart slammed against her ribs. Her throat tightened. She wanted to say *yes*, to make it easy, to be the girl everyone thought she was: lucky, grateful, perfect. The diamond sparkled between them, an unspoken promise of everything she had convinced herself she wanted. The life she could have with Jasper—the security, the prestige, the illusion of love—sat right there in that velvet box. It was beautiful, and for one aching moment, Cara wanted to believe in it. To believe that Jasper could be different, that his sharp edges could soften, that his love could become the kind she had always hoped it would be.

But that belief had always been more fragile than she admitted. It wavered under the weight of her doubts, cracked under the memory of his clipped words, cold silences, and hands grabbing her just a little bit too hard. She thought of the times she'd told herself it was her fault, that she just wasn't doing enough to make him happy. The moments when she had ignored the voice in her head whispering that love shouldn't feel like this.

Tears burned at the edges of her vision as the truth settled over her like a heavy, suffocating blanket. She wasn't just saying no to Jasper; she was letting go of the dream she'd clung to for too long—the dream that he could love her the way she wanted, the way she deserved. And it broke something deep inside her.

Her hands trembled as she searched his face, finding only expectation, not understanding. Not love. The weight of his gaze pressed down on her, and with it came fear—fear of what would happen when the answer she had to give left her lips. Fear of the anger that was always simmering beneath his charm.

"I..." she began, her voice breaking as the tears fell freely now. She shook her head, her chest tightening as if the air itself was turning against her. "I can't."

Jasper's expression didn't shift immediately. For a moment, he looked as if he hadn't heard her. Then, slowly, the smile slipped from his face. "What do you mean, you can't?"

"I mean no," she said, her voice firmer now, though the ache in her chest was unbearable. "I'm sorry, Jasper, but I can't marry you."

The silence that followed was deafening.

Jasper stood, his movements slow, deliberate. His face was a mask of calm, but his eyes burned with something dark and familiar in the way it made Cara tremble slightly. "You don't mean that," he said, his voice low. "You're just overwhelmed. This is a big moment."

Cara stepped back, shaking her head. "I do mean it. I'm sorry."

For a second, she thought he might yell, might let the mask slip entirely. His hand tightened around the velvet box, his knuckles going white, but then he laughed—a short, bitter sound that sent another chill down her spine. "You're making a mistake, Cara," he said, his voice low and cold, each word cutting into her like a razor. "But don't worry. You'll realize it. You'll come crawling back when you figure out what your life looks like without me."

She opened her mouth to respond, but no words came. The air in the room felt heavy, suffocating, as his gaze lingered on her for a moment longer, his lips curving into a smile that didn't reach his eyes. It wasn't warmth or love in that smile—it was a warning, a reminder of who he was and how little he thought of her.

Jasper turned, his movements slow and deliberate, as if giving her one last chance to stop him. She didn't. Her breath caught as he reached for the bottle of Dom Pérignon on her desk, lifting it with casual ease. "I'll take this," he said, his tone smooth but laced with venom. "No sense in wasting it on someone who doesn't know how to appreciate it."

His words hung in the air, cutting through the silence like shards of glass. She watched as he walked to the door, pausing with his hand on the frame. Without looking back, he said, "You'll regret this, Cara. Sooner than you think."

And then he was gone, the door clicking shut behind him, leaving her alone in the oppressive stillness of the room.

Cara sank onto her bed, her body trembling as the weight of what she had done crashed over her. She pressed her hands to her face, her sobs muffled by her palms. She was heartbroken, but not for the reason everyone would assume. She wasn't heartbroken because she had lost Jasper.

She was heartbroken because this was the first time, she had chosen herself, and it had been long overdue.

The Heart Was Yours To Break

The morning sunlight streamed through the blinds, but it did nothing to warm the hollow ache in Cara's chest. She hadn't slept—not really. Her body had been still, curled on the edge of her bed, but her mind had raced through the same thoughts over and over. What had she done? How could she have said no? Jasper had been everything she was supposed to want— everything she was told she should want. And now, she had thrown it all away.

Her chest tightened, and tears pricked her eyes as she stared at the ceiling. Maybe she *was* too much—too picky, too demanding, too unwilling to let go of the impossible idea of love she had carried with her since she was a girl. Jasper had told her as much, in small ways, over the years. That she expected perfection. That she didn't appreciate what she had. And maybe he was right. Maybe this was all her fault.

A knock at the door startled her, and she flinched instinctively, pulling her knees to her chest. The sound came again, more insistent this time. Cara wiped her face quickly and stood, her movements slow and hesitant. She didn't want to open the door. She didn't want to face anyone. But she couldn't avoid it forever.

When she opened the door, Rachel stood on the other side, her expression a mix of curiosity and something sharper—something almost angry. "Cara," she said, stepping inside without hesitation. "I heard about last night." Her voice carried the weight of accusation, her eyes scanning Cara like she was searching for answers.

Cara's stomach twisted. Of course Rachel had heard—Jasper's charm and their picture-perfect relationship had always been the stuff of campus legend. But Rachel's tone, her demeanour, made Cara's breath catch in her throat. Rachel wasn't just curious. She was furious.

Rachel crossed the room and sat on the edge of Cara's bed, her posture stiff. "You said no?" she asked, her voice low but sharp with disbelief. "To Jasper? Are you insane? Everyone's going to be talking about this, Cara. He's—" she paused, as if the word itself carried its own weight, "—devastated."

Cara's heart sank at the word, but it was Rachel's tone—biting and bafflingly cold—that cut the deepest. Rachel didn't understand. Rachel couldn't understand. They had grown up together in Jim Thorpe, Pennsylvania, dreaming about lives bigger than the ones they'd left behind. They'd come to Lehigh together, and through every step of university, Rachel had been by her side. Now, Cara wasn't sure who was sitting in front of her.

"I didn't mean to hurt him," Cara said softly, her voice barely above a whisper. She lowered her gaze, unwilling to meet Rachel's accusing stare. "It just... wasn't the right choice for me."

Rachel blinked, as though Cara had just spoken a foreign language. "The right choice?" she echoed, incredulous. "Cara, he's *Jasper*. Do you have any idea how many girls would kill to be in your position? He's gorgeous, he's rich, and he loves you. What more could you possibly want?"

Cara felt each word like a blow, her throat tightening as tears threatened to spill. She didn't answer—not because she didn't have an answer, but because her own doubts were already screaming the same questions inside her head. Rachel's words only added weight to the guilt and confusion she couldn't shake.

Rachel stood abruptly, brushing imaginary dust from her skirt with a sharp sigh. "You know everyone's going to be talking about this," she said. "Jasper's crushed, and you—" She cut herself off, her lips pressing into a thin line. "Honestly, Cara, I don't even know what to say to you. What were you thinking?"

The words struck harder than Cara expected, and she flinched under the weight of Rachel's tone. "I didn't mean—" Cara started, but the words faltered on her lips. She couldn't explain, not to Rachel. Not when Rachel had already made up her mind.

Rachel sighed again, shaking her head, her frustration palpable. "I've already talked to everyone this morning, Cara. Everyone knows. Jasper's *devastated*—he told us all everything. Or, well, as much as he could bring himself to say. God, he didn't even need to say much. The look on his face alone..." She trailed off, her voice trembling slightly before hardening again. "And now everyone's talking about how you turned him down. Do you know how bad this makes him look? How bad this makes *you* look?"

Cara's stomach twisted at the thought of Jasper—his charm, his magnetism—spinning their story just enough to make her into the villain. She could picture it so clearly: the pained expression, the soft, carefully chosen words that would inspire sympathy and outrage in equal measure. And, of course, everyone would believe him. Why wouldn't they? He was Jasper. Perfect, golden, faultless Jasper.

"I didn't mean to hurt him," she whispered, her voice barely audible. Her hands fidgeted with the hem of her pajama top; her knuckles white. "I just... it wasn't the right choice for me."

Rachel's incredulous laugh cut through the room like a blade. "The right choice?" she repeated, her voice dripping with disdain. "What does that even mean, Cara? He's Jasper. He loves you. He wanted to marry you. You had everything, and you just threw it away. For what?"

"I don't know," Cara admitted, her voice breaking as tears welled in her eyes. "I don't know, Rachel. I just—"

"Do you have any idea what you've done to him?" Rachel interrupted; her tone sharp. "To all of us? Everyone's talking about how selfish you are. How ungrateful. And I—" She broke off, shaking her head as if trying to make sense of it herself. "I don't get it. I really don't."

Cara flinched under Rachel's words, the guilt she had been trying to suppress bubbling to the surface. Her heart ached at the thought of Jasper hurt, at the image of him sitting with their friends, his head in his hands, his voice cracking as he tried to explain her rejection. She knew she shouldn't feel this way—she knew Jasper's pain was not her responsibility—but the weight of it pressed down on her anyway.

"I'm sorry," Cara said, the words spilling out in a desperate attempt to make it stop. "I didn't mean to hurt anyone. I just... I didn't know what else to do."

Rachel stared at her, her lips pressed into a tight line. "Yeah," she said finally, her voice flat. "You didn't know what else to do, so you broke him. And for what? To prove something to yourself? I hope it was worth it."

The words hit Cara like a slap, and she recoiled, tears slipping down her cheeks. Rachel didn't soften. She stood abruptly, brushing her skirt as though shaking off the conversation. "you're fucked in the head," she said coldly before walking out, letting the door slam shut behind her.

Cara sank onto her bed, the sound of the door slamming ringing in her ears. She clutched her hands to her chest, her sobs muffled as she doubled over. Rachel was right about one thing—everyone would believe Jasper. Everyone already had. And now, Cara was alone.

And worst of all, she couldn't stop the guilt that gnawed at her insides. The way she had hurt him—disappointed him—made her stomach churn. She knew she shouldn't feel this way. She knew, deep down, that Jasper wasn't the man everyone thought he was. But she couldn't bring herself to hate him, no matter how much she wanted to.

He deserved the admiration he got, didn't he? The adoration. The respect. He had been good to her, hadn't he? There were moments—moments she clung to—when he had been kind, generous, loving. Those moments had to mean something. Didn't they?

She buried her face in her hands, her shoulders shaking. No matter how much relief she had felt in the moment she said *no*, that relief was gone now, drowned under the weight of doubt and blame. She didn't want anyone to see Jasper for who he truly was—the way he had controlled her, chipped away at her confidence, and left her doubting her own worth. That wasn't who he was to everyone else, and it wasn't who she wanted him to be, either. He didn't deserve that. He didn't deserve to lose the admiration of their friends, the pedestal he had worked so hard to stand on.

Now, she had upset everything—the delicate balance of their group, the expectations everyone had placed on her, the version of herself they all believed in. She had let them down. She had let Jasper down. And the pressure of all of it was suffocating.

The dorm bathroom was small and clinical, with harsh fluorescent lights that buzzed faintly overhead. Cara started the shower and stepped under the stream of water, letting it pour over her, hot enough to sting. She kept her eyes shut, willing the water to wash away the weight pressing down on her chest. The relief she'd felt last night, in the brief moment of saying no, had all but evaporated. All that was left was the nagging guilt, the feeling that she had ruined everything.

As the water streamed down her body, Cara's gaze fell to her arm, and her breath caught. Just above her elbow, faint bruises were beginning to bloom—soft smudges of blue and yellow against her skin. She brushed her fingers over them lightly, wincing at the tenderness. It hadn't registered at the time, not fully. But now, in the stark clarity of morning, the memory came back to her.

It had happened on the dance floor, before everything had unravelled. Jasper had leaned in close, his lips brushing her ear, his voice low and controlled. "Let's go," he had said, his hand resting on her waist. She'd hesitated, wanting just one more dance, just a few more moments to linger in the magic of the night. When she told him so, her words had been careful, measured. But his hand had tightened, his fingers digging in—not enough to hurt, not quite, but enough to make his displeasure clear. He hadn't argued. He hadn't said a word. He had simply walked away, leaving her there on the dance floor, her face burning under the weight of what felt like failure.

Now, staring at the bruise, Cara's stomach churned. Her mind circled the memory like a moth to a flame, drawn to every detail: the way the lights of the ballroom had seemed to dim when he left, the way she had stood frozen for a moment, unsure whether to follow him or stay. And she had stayed. She had kept dancing.

Her fingers traced the outline of the bruise as her chest tightened. It was no wonder things had gone so wrong. She had let go of him on the dance floor, in more ways than one. She hadn't been the partner he needed her to be. If she had just left with him when he asked, maybe the night would have ended differently. Maybe she wouldn't have let him down so completely.

Cara pressed her forehead against the cool tiles, the water cascading around her as shame twisted in her chest. She scrubbed at her arm with more force than necessary, as though she could erase the bruise, erase her mistakes. But the guilt stayed, clinging to her like the steam in the air. She should have known. She should have been better.

The water ran cold before she turned it off, shivering as she stepped out of the shower. Back in her dorm room, Cara dried herself off, her hands trembling as she moved to her closet. It was packed with clothes Jasper had chosen for her, each piece carefully selected and gifted with his approval. She had always thought of it as thoughtful, even sweet, the way he took such an interest in her appearance. He'd tell her which colours suited her best, which cuts flattered her figure, which outfits she shouldn't be seen in. "You deserve to look your best," he'd say, his voice so soft and full of conviction that Cara had never thought to question him.

She pulled a blouse from its hanger, pale blue with delicate stitching along the collar. Jasper had chosen it for her last fall, saying it matched her eyes. She dressed slowly, slipping on dark jeans and clasping a gold necklace around her neck—another gift from him, this one for her birthday. Her reflection in the mirror was polished, perfect. It was exactly how he liked her to look. For a moment, her lips curved into the faintest smile as she adjusted the necklace. Maybe if she could hold onto this version of herself —the one he had shaped so carefully—she could convince herself she wasn't the problem.

But the smile faded as quickly as it had appeared, and Cara turned away from the mirror, her chest tightening. She grabbed her bag and moved toward the door, her hand pausing on the handle. Rachel's words from earlier echoed in her mind. *Everyone knows.*

The thought made her stomach twist. She could already feel the stares, the judgment, the whispers that would follow her everywhere she went. They would all believe Jasper's version of the story. They would all believe his heartbreak and they would all blame her for it. They would see her as ungrateful, as selfish, as the girl who had dropped the hand of the man every other girl on campus would have clung to for life. And the worst part was, she wasn't even sure they were wrong.

Taking a shaky breath, Cara opened the door and stepped into the hallway. The walk to the closest campus coffee kiosk felt endless, her head down and her shoulders hunched as though she could shield herself from the world's gaze. But it didn't matter. Every glance felt like an accusation, every murmured voice like a judgment.

"She actually said no. Can you believe it?"

"Poor Jasper. I heard he's devastated."

"What's *wrong* with her?"

The words hung in the air like smoke, suffocating and inescapable. Cara clutched her bag tighter, and kept walking, willing herself not to cry. She didn't know what she would do once she reached the coffee kiosk, or what she would do after that. She didn't know how she was going to face her parents when she returned home to Jim Thorpe tomorrow, feeling sure they adored Jasper and would see her decision as a betrayal. All she knew was that there was no escaping this—not here, not at home, not anywhere.

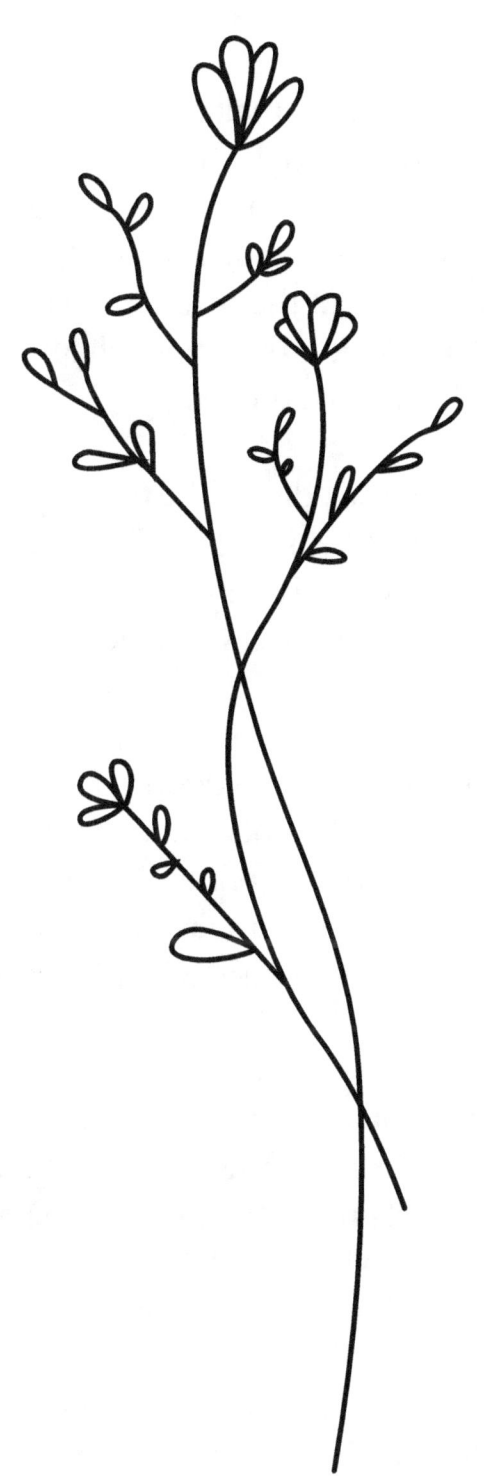

The Beginning Of Us

Cara's coffee sat untouched on the small wooden table, the steam curling up in faint tendrils before fading into the air. She stared at it blankly, her mind too scattered to even consider taking a sip. Around her, campus had begun to hum with more quiet chatter and the soft hiss of the espresso machine from the coffee kiosk, but the sounds blurred into an indistinct hum in her ears. Every glance in her direction felt like a spotlight, every muffled laugh a private joke at her expense.

Her fingers tightened around the edge of the table, grounding herself against the storm in her chest. She thought of Rachel's voice, sharp and unforgiving, and the murmurs she'd heard as she walked here. They all believed she had thrown away something perfect. And there was a part of her that believed that too.

As she sat there, the memory came unbidden, rushing in like the tide. She could still see the library, where she had spent so much of her time at Lehigh, rows of towering bookshelves bathed in golden afternoon light. It had been her first year, and she'd been searching for a book she couldn't find, her nerves frayed from the pressure of a midterm looming just days away.

"Political theory, huh? Ambitious," a warm voice had said, startling her. She had turned to find a tall, striking figure standing at the end of the aisle, his dark hair catching the sunlight as though it had been placed there just for him to stand in. He had a smile that felt like an invitation, and his sharp green eyes had sparkled with curiosity as they met hers.

"I guess," she'd replied awkwardly, hugging her notebook to her chest as if it might shield her from the intensity of his gaze. She'd never been good at small talk, and her cheeks flushed under his attention.

He stepped closer, holding out a book she hadn't noticed he was carrying. "Is this what you're looking for?"

It had been. She stared at the book, then back at him, a little stunned. "Yes... How did you know?"

"You looked determined and slightly lost. I took a guess," he'd said with a grin, his voice tinged with a quiet confidence that put her at ease despite herself.

She took the book from him carefully, her fingers brushing against his, and felt an unexpected jolt of electricity. "Thank you," she murmured.

"Anytime," he replied. "I'm Jasper, by the way."

That was how it started—something small and seemingly unremarkable, but it had felt like fate at the time. Jasper had swept into her life like a storybook prince, charming and attentive in ways she hadn't known she'd needed or wanted. Their first conversation in the library had stretched into hours, their shared laughter filling the spaces between them. He had listened to her dreams, her fears, her thoughts about things she hadn't even known she wanted to share. He made her feel seen, important, as though the world stopped when he looked at her.

It wasn't long before she had fallen for him completely. Jasper had swept her off her feet with grand gestures: flowers delivered to her dorm for no reason at all, expensive dinners at restaurants she couldn't pronounce, and handwritten notes tucked into her books, filled with words that made her heart race. He remembered the smallest details, the things she hadn't thought anyone noticed, and turned them into moments that felt magical. With him, she'd felt weightless, like the best version of herself. Everyone told her how lucky she was, and she believed it.

For so long, it was those early sparks she clung to—the warmth of his attention, the way he had looked at her like she was the only person in the room. Whenever things grew difficult, whenever his words turned sharp or his grip left faint marks on her arm, she would remind herself of who Jasper had been at the beginning. She was sure that was who he truly was, deep down, and that if she could just be better—less emotional, less difficult, less everything—then she could bring him back.

Now, sitting in the café with her coffee growing cold, Cara felt a lump rise in her throat. That Jasper—the one she'd fallen for—seemed like a distant dream. But she could still remember him. And sitting here now, she wondered if he was still in there somewhere, hidden beneath the sharp edges that had begun to show over the years.

The thought was a knife in her chest, twisting as she tried to reconcile the man she had loved with the man she had walked away from. If she had loved him once, hadn't that been enough? If she had held on tighter, could things have been different?

Cara swallowed hard, blinking back tears as she tore her gaze away from her untouched coffee. No, she told herself firmly. She couldn't keep thinking like this. But even as she tried to push the memories away, they lingered, soft and painful, like the faint echo of a song she couldn't forget.

Rachel's words echoed in her mind like a refrain she couldn't escape: "You're fucked in the head."

Maybe she was.

Tears pricked at Cara's eyes. What if Rachel was right? What if Jasper had been right? She had broken everything—her relationship, her friendships, and maybe herself. The knot in her stomach twisted tighter with every passing thought. She tried to push them away, but they came rushing back with the force of a tide. Had she made the biggest mistake of her life? Should she have said yes? Should she have gone back to him already, begged him to forgive her for being so selfish?

Her chest ached as her mind drifted to one of the memories she clung to most—one of those moments when everything had felt perfect, when Jasper had been perfect.

It was their three-month anniversary, something Cara had never celebrated with any other partner in her life. It had felt like a small milestone, not something to make a fuss over. But Jasper had swept her into a whirlwind of romance and insisted it was important. "Every moment is worth celebrating," he had told her as they strolled through the sprawling gardens of a historic estate just outside Bethlehem. The sun was setting, painting the sky in hues of orange and pink, and Jasper had arranged for a private dinner in the estate's courtyard, complete with string lights, soft music, and a table set for two.

Cara had felt like she was in a movie. The candles flickered in the soft breeze as they ate, Jasper filling the conversation with talk of their future together. He painted vivid pictures of their life to come: a beautiful home, children who would inherit their best qualities, grandchildren they'd spoil rotten. "I can't wait to sit with you in our garden one day," he'd said, his hand warm over hers, "and tell our grandchildren all about this—about how it all began."

Her heart had swelled at his words. No one had ever spoken to her like that before, with such certainty about the future, with such confidence that she was the one. She had laughed, a little shyly, and told him how incredible he made her feel.

But the evening had taken a subtle turn as dessert was served—tiny, elaborate cakes on delicate porcelain plates. Cara had made a small joke about how the desserts looked too perfect to eat, but Jasper's smile had tightened ever so slightly.

"You know, not everything has to be a joke," he'd said lightly, but the edge in his voice made her falter.

"I didn't mean anything by it," she had replied quickly, her cheeks burning.

Jasper leaned back in his chair, his expression neutral, but there was something about the way he looked at her that made her heart sink. "You can be so dismissive sometimes," he'd said softly, shaking his head like it hurt him more than it hurt her. "I went to a lot of trouble to make this night special for you, Cara."

His words had stung more than she'd expected. She'd tried to recover, apologizing and assuring him she appreciated everything he had done, but the lump in her throat refused to dissolve. Tears pricked her eyes as they continued the evening, the lightness between them replaced by something tense and fragile. Later, on the car ride home, Jasper had taken her hand and smiled at her, as if the moment had never happened. But it had.

Even now, the memory of that night twisted in her chest. She had thought it was her fault—had told herself over and over that she should have known better than to make the joke. Jasper had put so much effort into making her feel special, and she had ruined it with a thoughtless comment. He deserved someone who appreciated him more, someone who didn't make stupid mistakes and dumb jokes.

Now, Cara blinked back the tears threatening to spill and her fingers played with the plastic lid of her coffee. Maybe she *was* the problem. Maybe Rachel was right. Maybe Jasper was right. And maybe the only thing she needed to do now was admit it—and find a way to fix it.

Almost Family

Cara picked up her coffee, its warmth a small comfort against the cold that had settled deep in her chest. She didn't even care that it had gone lukewarm—it gave her something to hold onto as she walked back to her dorm, her head down, her steps measured. The whispers still followed her, lingering like smoke in the air, but she forced herself not to turn around. Not to react. She just needed to get back to her room.

When she closed the door behind her, the silence of her dorm felt almost deafening. She set the coffee down on her desk, staring at the cluttered space as her thoughts churned. The idea of staying here, even for one more day, felt unbearable. On impulse, she reached for her phone and scrolled through her contacts until she found the one labelled Home. Her thumb hovered over the name for a moment before she tapped it, her stomach twisting as the line rang.

"Cara!" her mother's voice came through the line, warm and cheerful. "I wasn't expecting to hear from you so soon. How are you, darling?"

"I'm okay," Cara said softly, though her voice cracked on the last word. She paused, swallowing hard before continuing. "Actually, I was wondering... would it be alright if I came home early? I just... I think I need to leave campus sooner than I planned."

"Of course," her mother said immediately, her tone tinged with concern. "You don't even have to ask. Come home whenever you're ready. Your father and I would love to have you here a day early. The sooner, the better!"

Cara's chest tightened at the kindness in her mother's voice, and she blinked back tears. "Thanks, Mom," she whispered. "I'll probably head out in a bit."

"Do you need us to come help you pack?" her mother asked.

"No, I've got it all finished already," Cara said quickly, shaking her head even though her mother couldn't see her. "Jasper helped me. Thank you, though."

After hanging up, Cara set the phone down and stared at the room around her. It wasn't much—just a tiny private dorm that she had initially resisted but had ended up accepting because Jasper insisted. He had wanted somewhere private just for them, away from prying eyes and shared spaces. Jasper had paid for it without hesitation, calling it "an investment in their future," while he himself lived in a townhouse provided by his parents, sharing it with his older sister. At the time, it had felt like a generous gesture, a way to make her life easier, but now, standing in the quiet stillness of the room, it felt like another thing that wasn't truly hers. She grabbed a box from the corner of the room and began heading for her car.

Her car sat waiting for her in the parking lot—a sleek, silver Audi A4, just a few years old. Cara hadn't wanted such a nice car to replace her old Chevrolet Chevette; she had grown up in Jim Thorpe, Pennsylvania, where cars were practical, not flashy. But when she and Jasper had been dating for a year, his parents—Reginald and Victoria Whitmore—had insisted on helping her buy something. "You're practically family, Cara," Victoria had said with a warm smile, her diamond earrings catching the light as she sipped her tea. "It's the least we can do for our future daughter-in-law."

At the time, Cara had blushed and protested, insisting she couldn't let them spend so much on her. "I'll just get something used," she'd said, her voice shy. But the Whitmores had exchanged a look, as if her modesty were quaint but misguided.

"Nonsense," Reginald had said, his deep voice carrying the weight of authority. "A young woman like you needs something safe, reliable—something worthy of you."

They had taken her to a Mercedes dealership, pointing out the newest models with all the latest features. But Cara had been firm, shaking her head at every suggestion. "Thank you so much," she had said, her cheeks burning, "but I really can't let you do that. I'll find something nice and practical."

In the end, they had compromised on the Audi, though it had still felt far more luxurious than anything she'd ever imagined driving. Jasper had been quiet during the whole ordeal, his smile tight, his hand gripping hers just a little too firmly. She thought he was annoyed with his parents' insistence, but later, she realized his frustration had been with her.

The first time she drove the car to campus, Jasper had offered to park it for her. She had handed him the keys with a smile, thinking he was being sweet, but when she asked for them back later, he had held them just out of reach.

"Don't you think you should be thanking me properly for this?" he had said, his tone light but his grip on her wrist firm. Her laughter had faltered, unsure if he was joking. When she tried to take the keys again, his hand tightened, pulling her closer. "I mean it, Cara. You embarrassed me in front of my parents. Do you know how that made me look?"

His words had stung, and when she apologized softly, tears welling in her eyes, he had sighed and pressed the keys into her hand firmly, squeezing her fist closed around them until she whimpered. "It's fine," he had said, his voice cool as he let her go. "Just don't do it again."

Even now, as she loaded boxes into the trunk of the Audi, the memory lingered, sharp and bitter. She had thought, at the time, that she'd overreacted—that she'd been too sensitive, too quick to take things personally. Standing here now, under the glare of the late-afternoon sun, she still wasn't sure she'd been wrong. Maybe Jasper had been right to call her out. She had embarrassed him in front of his parents, after all. They had been so kind, so welcoming, treating her like family long before she truly was. The knot of guilt tightened in her stomach, making her chest feel heavy. It was her fault, wasn't it? All of it—if she had just been better, quieter, more grateful—things wouldn't have turned out this way.

She paused, her hand resting on the edge of the open trunk, and let the thought she'd been trying to push away finally take root: Was she making another mistake now? Should she really be driving back to her parents' house, where questions and judgment about her decision to leave Jasper would surely wait for her? Or should she be going to Jasper's townhouse to apologize—to beg Jasper to forgive her? She could still fix this. Couldn't she? If she showed him how sorry she was, if she told him she'd been overwhelmed and confused, he might take her back. He loved her, didn't he? He'd said they were meant to be, that they would be together forever. She could call him. She could drive to him. She could take back her answer and say *yes*.

Her heart pounded as the idea bloomed, both terrifying and reassuring all at once. Maybe she could undo the damage she'd caused. Maybe it wasn't too late.

On her final trip to the car, balancing a box full of books and a duffel bag slung over her shoulder, Cara nearly ran into a figure rounding the corner of the dorm parking lot.

"Cara?" the girl said, her tone dripping with incredulity. "Wow, I didn't think I'd run into you here."

Cara blinked, recognizing the sharp voice and perfectly styled blonde hair immediately. It was Arabella, one of Jasper's closest friends—someone who always seemed to be lingering in the background of his life, dressed in head-to-toe designer and wielding her sharp tongue like a weapon. Arabella wasn't someone Cara had spent much time with, but her presence was hard to forget.

"Oh," Cara said, shifting her weight awkwardly under the weight of the box. "Hi, Arabella."

Arabella's perfectly sculpted brows arched as she looked Cara up and down, her lips curling into a faint smirk. "Packing up already? Well, I guess that makes sense. It's not like you'd want to stick around after what happened." Her tone was light, almost amused, but her words hit Cara like a punch to the stomach.

Cara's heart sank, and she set the box down on the edge of the trunk, trying to steady herself. "What do you mean?" she asked, though she already knew the answer.

"Oh, come on, Cara," Arabella said with a laugh that felt like nails on a chalkboard. "Everyone knows. You broke up with Jasper. I mean, I've heard of cold feet, but this is something else. What was it Rachel said?" She tapped her manicured nails against her lips, pretending to think. "'Fucked in the head'? Yeah, that sounds about right."

Cara flinched, the words cutting deeper than she wanted to admit. "I—" she began, but Arabella didn't let her finish.

"Honestly, though, I don't know what you were thinking. Jasper's incredible. But hey, maybe it's for the best. He seems to be moving on just fine." Arabella's smirk widened, her eyes glittering with something cruel. "I saw him this morning, actually. He was leaving Lydia Harrington's apartment. You know her, right? They've been close forever—practically grew up together. She's always adored him. Guess now she's finally getting her chance."

The blood drained from Cara's face. She knew Lydia—had known her since Jasper had introduced them early in their relationship. Lydia was beautiful, elegant in the effortless way Cara could never be, and she had always seemed to hover just at the edges of Jasper's life. Cara had felt threatened by her from the start, though Jasper had always dismissed her concerns. "Lydia's like a sister to me," he'd say with a laugh, brushing off her worries as if they were ridiculous. But Cara had never been able to shake the feeling that Lydia wanted more.

Arabella laughed again, flipping her hair over her shoulder. "Honestly, it kind of serves you right. You led him on for years, and now you're surprised he's moving on? Please."

Cara felt her throat tighten, tears threatening to spill, but she forced herself to keep her voice steady. "Thanks for letting me know," she said quietly, turning back to the trunk and shoving the box inside with more force than necessary.

Arabella shrugged. "Anytime. Good luck, Cara," she said, her voice dripping with false sweetness as she walked away.

As Cara climbed into the driver's seat of the Audi, her mind raced with memories, one in particular rising to the surface with painful clarity. It had been a year and three months into her relationship with Jasper, and as always, he had planned something elaborate to celebrate their anniversary. Every month they had marked the occasion with grand gestures, but this time, Jasper had promised her something even more special—a surprise that he had refused to give any details about. Cara had spent the day giddy with excitement, carefully choosing her outfit and imagining what he had planned.

But as the evening approached, Jasper still hadn't arrived to pick her up. She had called him once, then twice, her heart sinking with each unanswered ring. Hours passed, and finally, her phone buzzed with a text: *Can't make it tonight. Something came up. We'll talk later.*

It wasn't until days later that she found out what had "come up." Jasper had spent the evening with Lydia. Cara hadn't known at first, but social media had a way of filling in the gaps. A picture of them at a private art gallery opening, Lydia beaming up at him, had been enough to break Cara's heart. When she confronted Jasper about it, he shrugged it off.

"Celebrating every month is so... trivial," he had said, his tone dismissive. "We're not kids, Cara. I didn't think it was that big of a deal."

"But you said—" Cara had begun, her voice trembling, but Jasper had cut her off.

"You shouldn't have gotten your hopes up," he had said, his voice cool. "I can't drop everything for something so silly. Don't be so dramatic."

The memory twisted in her chest like a knife as she gripped the steering wheel, her knuckles white. Arabella's words about Lydia echoed in her mind, sharp and mocking. Jasper had always had a way of making her feel small, of turning her hurt into something trivial. And yet, she had always forgiven him, always convinced herself that it wasn't his fault—that it was hers.

Cara blinked back tears, staring at the road ahead. The thought of driving to his townhouse, of seeing him, of trying to patch things up, made her stomach churn. Maybe Arabella was right—maybe Jasper had already moved on. Maybe he had never really been hers to begin with.

She turned the key in the ignition, the Audi purring to life beneath her. She couldn't go to him. Not now. Not after everything. Her only choice was to go home—to her parents, to Jim Thorpe, to the only place where she could try to make sense of the relationship and Jasper's heart of glass that she had shattered to pieces.

The road stretched ahead of her, winding through the rolling hills and dense forests of eastern Pennsylvania. The trees stood like sentinels, their branches stretching toward the clear spring sky. The closer Cara got to Jim Thorpe, the more the landscape shifted into something almost picturesque—old farmhouses with weathered shutters, curling smoke from brick chimneys, and the quiet stillness of spring creeping in.

The Audi hummed steadily beneath her, the soft purr of the engine the only sound in the cocoon of the car. She passed a creek that wound through the woods, the water dark and restless as it rushed over smooth stones. It was the kind of scene that always reminded her of home.

Her thoughts drifted, unbidden, to a Thanksgiving two years ago. She had been with Jasper for two years then, and he had invited her to spend the holiday with his family at their estate in the Poconos. Cara had hesitated at first, nervous about being a part of such an intimate gathering, but Jasper had brushed her concerns aside. "You're part of the family," he'd said, his green eyes warm and reassuring. "They'll love having you there."

The estate was grand, a sprawling house perched on the edge of a frozen lake. Snow dusted the manicured lawns, and icicles clung to the edges of the slate roof like delicate crystal ornaments. Inside, a fire roared in the massive stone hearth, casting a golden glow across the polished floors and high ceilings. Jasper's parents were as gracious as always. His father gave her a tour of the property, after which, his mother insisted on sitting Cara down for tea, fussing over her like she was already part of the family. His cousins, Charlotte and Henry, had greeted her warmly, and Victoria's sister and her husband were equally kind. The entire scene had felt plucked from a holiday movie.

Dinner that evening was held in the formal dining room, the long table set with fine china and gleaming silver candelabras. The scent of roasted turkey, spiced cranberry sauce, and freshly baked bread filled the air as the family laughed and shared stories over wine. Cara had been seated next to Jasper, his hand resting lightly on her thigh under the table. It had felt perfect, like a moment she could have stepped into and stayed in forever.

But then, it had happened.

She hadn't meant to say anything wrong. It had been a lighthearted comment, a small joke about how Jasper had packed mismatched gloves for their trip, something that had made her laugh earlier. She'd thought it was harmless, but the moment the words left her mouth, she felt the shift. Jasper's smile froze, his fingers tensing on her leg.

"Not everything needs to be shared, Cara," he said lightly, but the edge in his voice was unmistakable, though no one else seemed to notice.

Cara's cheeks flushed, and she opened her mouth to apologize, but before she could, Jasper reached for his wine glass. The movement seemed careless, almost clumsy, but she knew better. The glass tipped, spilling deep red wine across her sweater and onto her lap.

The table fell silent as Cara gasped, grabbing at her sweater to blot the stain. "Oh no, I'm so sorry!" she stammered, her voice trembling.

Jasper let out a soft sigh, shaking his head. "Cara," he said, his tone gentle but tinged with exasperation. "You've had too much to drink. You need to be more careful."

"I didn't—" she started to protest, but Jasper was already standing, his hand on her arm as he helped her up.

"It's alright, everyone," he said, his sheepish smile directed at the others. "I'll take care of her." His voice was filled with concern, every move calculated to seem as though he were the perfect, attentive boyfriend.

Cara's throat tightened as she let him lead her upstairs, the wine-soaked sweater clinging to her skin. When they reached the guest room, Jasper shut the door behind them with a click, and the air in the room grew heavy.

"You embarrassed me," he said, his voice low and cold.

"I didn't mean to—" she started, her voice trembling, but he cut her off.

"Do you think it's funny to make me look bad in front of my family?" His words were sharp, and Cara felt each one like a blow.

Tears welled in her eyes as she shook her head. "No, Jasper, I swear I didn't —"

"Stop," he said, his voice rising slightly. His jaw tightened as he took a deliberate step toward her. She had already pulled off the wine-stained sweater and jeans, the damp fabric discarded on the floor. Standing there in just her underwear, shivering against the cold, she looked up at him, her cheeks wet with tears.

The slap wasn't hard—not enough to leave a mark, just a flushed redness on her cheek—but it was enough to make her stagger back, her breath hitching as shock coursed through her. She crumpled to the floor, curling into herself as silent sobs racked her body. The cold from the hardwood seeped into her skin, and she wrapped her arms around herself, trembling.

Minutes passed before she could speak. "I'm cold," she whispered, her voice barely audible.

Jasper's expression softened instantly, the anger melting away as if it had never been there. He crossed the room in two strides, grabbing one of his thick flannel shirts from the closet. "Oh, sweetheart," he murmured, kneeling beside her and draping the shirt over her shoulders. His hands were gentle, his voice warm and full of concern as he pulled her into his arms. "I'm so sorry. I didn't mean to scare you. You know I love you, don't you? I just get so frustrated sometimes."

Cara nodded, wiping away her tears with the sleeve of his flannel shirt as he pressed a kiss to her hair. "It's alright," she whispered, her voice trembling. "I'm sorry. I shouldn't have—"

"Shh," he said, his hand rubbing soothing circles on her back. "It's okay, my love. Let's go back downstairs. They'll understand."

When they returned to the dining room, Cara was wrapped in Jasper's flannel, her hair let down to disguise her tear-streaked face. "Sorry about that," she said softly, forcing a smile as she looked around the table. "The wine went straight to my head."

Jasper squeezed her hand as they sat back down, his charming smile back in place as the conversation resumed. Beneath the table, his fingers rested lightly on her leg.

The memory clung to her as the road stretched on beneath her tires, the Audi's engine steady. At the time, she had believed Jasper's version of events—that the spilled wine, the slap, everything—had somehow been her fault. She had sat back at the table and apologized as though she were the one who needed forgiveness.

But now, with the freedom of the road stretching out in front of her, the memory felt different. She gripped the steering wheel tighter, her brow furrowing. Maybe it wasn't her fault. Maybe she hadn't deserved any of it. And maybe—just maybe—saying *no* to Jasper the previous night had been the first thing she had done right in a long time.

The thought flickered in her mind like a small, stubborn flame, refusing to go out. She wasn't sure if she believed it yet, but for the first time, she let herself wonder.

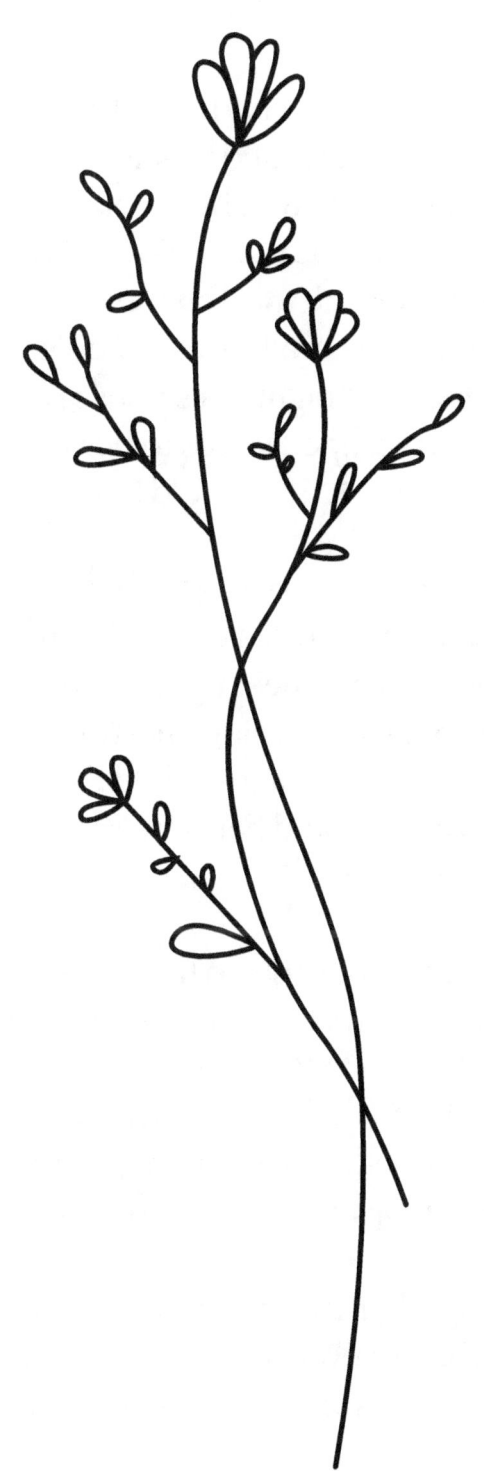

The Unravelling

The house came into view as Cara turned onto the quiet street she had grown up on, and for the first time that day, she felt a flicker of relief. It wasn't exactly a haven, not with the weight of her decision still pressing down on her, but it was familiar. The pale yellow siding, the garden her mother had always fussed over, the wind chime made from sea glass that danced gently in the breeze—it was all a welcome sight after the chaos that had filled her mind since last night. This house had seen her through every phase of her life, from scraped knees to her first heartbreak. And now, she was here again, hoping it might hold her together one more time.

Her mother must have seen her car pulling into the driveway, because the front door opened just as Cara stepped out of the Audi. The warmth of her mother's expression made Cara's chest tighten. She hadn't expected it— hadn't expected anything but the looming question of what her parents would say when they learned everything. Would they tell her she was crazy for walking away? Would they remind her how lucky she'd been to have Jasper in the first place?

"Cara!" her mother called, stepping down from the porch. The warmth in her voice and the sight of her familiar figure standing against the backdrop of the house—the place that had always felt safe—nearly broke her. Cara climbed out of the car, but before she could say a word, her mother's face shifted from cheerful to worried, her brows knitting together as she took in the tears already spilling down Cara's cheeks.

"Sweetheart, what's wrong?" her mother asked, her voice soft with concern as she crossed the driveway to meet her. Without waiting for a response, she wrapped Cara in her arms, holding her tightly.

The touch undid her completely. Cara dissolved into sobs, her breath hitching as the emotions she'd been holding back flooded out of her. Her mother didn't press her, just held her close, murmuring soothing words into her hair. "It's okay, baby. Let's go inside," she said gently, leading Cara up the porch steps and through the front door.

The warmth of the house, the familiar scent of coffee and cinnamon lingering in the air, made Cara's chest tighten further. Her mother guided her to the couch, her worry deepening as she brushed a strand of hair from Cara's face. "Sweetheart, tell me what happened. Is it school? Did something happen on campus?" she asked softly.

Cara shook her head, her tears still falling, her hands gripping the edge of her sweater. Her mother sat beside her, one hand resting gently on her knee. "Take your time," she said, her voice steady.

Cara stared at the floor, her heart pounding as she tried to force the words out. "Jasper proposed," she said finally, her voice cracking on the last word. She swallowed hard, blinking rapidly as she braced herself for what came next. "And I... I said no."

Her mother's face registered surprise, but she didn't say anything. Cara's voice grew quieter as she continued, the words tumbling out in a rush. "He asked me last night, and I couldn't—I just couldn't say yes. I told him no, and now everyone thinks I'm insane. Rachel told me I was crazy. And maybe I am, Mom. Maybe I am."

Her mother's eyes softened as she reached for Cara's hands, holding them tightly in her own. "Oh, sweetheart," she said, her tone gentle but firm. "You are not crazy. But tell me—why couldn't you say yes?"

Cara hesitated, her chest tightening. She had never told her parents the truth about Jasper—never wanted them to see the cracks in the perfect image everyone believed in. But sitting here now, her mother's steady gaze fixed on her, the words felt like they were clawing their way out of her throat.

"Because of how he makes me feel," Cara whispered finally. Her voice broke as she continued, her words faltering. "Because of the way he talks to me... the way he grabs me when he's angry... the way he makes me feel like I'm not enough, no matter how hard I try to be. I couldn't say yes because I know, deep down, that it's not right. That he's not right."

Her mother's face paled, her lips pressing into a thin line. She opened her mouth to respond, but Cara shook her head quickly, her tears falling faster now. "But I don't know if I made a mistake. What if I ruined everything? What if he's right, and I'm just too difficult to love?"

"Oh, Cara," her mother said softly, pulling her into another embrace. "Sweetheart, no. No. It's not you. It's not your fault. You didn't ruin anything by saying no. You did the right thing—do you hear me? You did the right thing for you, and that is who you should be worrying about."

Cara clung to her mother, the weight of her words settling over her like a blanket.

Cara sniffled, her tears slowing but still leaving her chest heavy. Her mother reached for the tissue box on the coffee table, pulling out a few and handing them to Cara. "Here, sweetheart," she said softly. Cara took the tissues with trembling hands, dabbing at her eyes and nose as her mother watched her, concern etched deeply into her features.

After a moment, her mother spoke, her tone tentative. "Cara, I need to tell you something. I don't want to upset you, but I think... I think you should know."

Cara glanced up, her breath catching in her throat. "What is it?"

Her mother hesitated, her hands folding in her lap as she gathered her thoughts. "Do you remember when Jasper visited us about a year ago? It was a long weekend. You didn't come with him because you had a big exam coming up, and you were staying on campus to study."

Cara frowned, trying to piece the memory together. She vaguely remembered Jasper visiting her parents alone, but she hadn't thought much of it at the time. "Yeah, I remember. What about it?"

"Well, he came here to ask your dad and me for permission to propose to you," her mother said, her voice low. "At first, I was touched. It seemed so traditional, so respectful. But then... I don't know, Cara. There was something about the way he said it, about the way he talked about you, that didn't sit right with me."

Cara's heart pounded in her chest. "What do you mean?"

Her mother sighed, her gaze dropping to her hands. "He didn't talk about you the way someone in love should. He talked about you like... like you were someone he needed to take care of, like a project. He said things like, 'Cara wouldn't know what to do without me,' or, 'She needs me to help her stay on track.' I remember feeling so uneasy, but I told myself I was overthinking it. You just seemed to happy."

Cara's stomach twisted as her mother continued.

"And then," her mother added, her voice growing softer, "there was this moment when we were having coffee in the kitchen. I'd baked muffins, and I offered him one. He took it, and the ones I asked him to take back to campus for you, but he made this little comment about how he hoped you wouldn't eat too many of them because 'Cara's always been sensitive about her weight.' He said it like it was nothing, like it wasn't a big deal. But it felt... wrong. It felt cruel."

Cara stared at her mother, her breath hitching. She remembered Jasper making comments like that before, always wrapped in a joking tone but cutting her deeply.

"You knew?" she asked softly, her voice trembling. "You... you don't think I am crazy for saying no?"

Her mother's face softened, her eyes glistening with unshed tears. "Oh, sweetheart, no. Never. I only wish I'd said something sooner. Your dad and I, we saw these little things, but we convinced ourselves we were imagining it. You seemed so happy, and we didn't want to ruin that for you. We didn't know how bad things were. But deep down... we hoped he wouldn't propose. We hoped you'd say no if he did."

Cara blinked, the weight of her mother's words sinking in. She had walked into this house prepared for disappointment, for judgment. Instead, she felt something she hadn't expected: relief. Her parents had seen it—maybe not all of it, but enough. They weren't angry with her. They weren't disappointed. They believed her.

Her mother squeezed her hand tightly. "I wish I'd trusted my instincts and said something back then. But I'm so proud of you, Cara. You did the right thing. You were brave."

Cara felt her chest tighten, but it wasn't from the same suffocating weight she had been carrying since the proposal. It was something else— something lighter. She wasn't sure she could believe it yet, not completely, but for the first time, the edges of her doubt began to blur. Maybe she had done the right thing. Maybe it hadn't been her fault. Maybe, just maybe, she had chosen something better.

What She Chose
Five Years Later

The biting December wind swept through the streets of Bethlehem as Cara pulled her coat tighter around her and adjusted the scarf around her neck. Christmas lights glinted off shop windows, their warm glow a stark contrast to the cold air that nipped at her cheeks. It was a far cry from the dry, sunny winters of Eagle Pass, Texas, where she now lived and worked. But despite the chill, there was something comforting about being home for the holidays—back in the cocoon of familiarity that Jim Thorpe provided.

Cara had arrived a few days earlier, spending time with her parents and enjoying the slower pace of life she rarely afforded herself. Most of her days were spent working tirelessly as an immigration lawyer in Eagle Pass, where she fought for families desperate to stay together, for people clinging to the hope of a better future. It wasn't glamorous work, and it was often emotionally draining, but it was hers. For the first time in her life, Cara felt like she was making a real difference—helping people in ways that mattered.

Her phone buzzed in her pocket, pulling her from her thoughts. It was Rachel, she was the one who had convinced Cara to take this little detour today.

"You're late," Rachel teased when Cara picked up.

"It's freezing," Cara replied with a laugh. "Remind me why we're doing this again?"

"Because it's tradition," Rachel said. "The alumni holiday thing at Lehigh is a classic, and we haven't been back in years. Plus, I promised to stop by the admin building to drop off some forms for that certification course I'm taking, remember? You're just here for moral support."

Cara sighed but couldn't help smiling. "Fine, fine. I'm on my way."

By the time she reached the Lehigh campus and met up with Rachel, it was alive with a festive energy. Wreaths adorned the doors of academic buildings, twinkling lights draped over lampposts, and a towering Christmas tree stood proudly in the main quad, its ornaments catching the soft glow of the late afternoon sun. The halls were bustling with alumni and current students, bundled in coats and scarves, their voices echoing through the corridors. Walking through those familiar hallways felt strange, almost surreal. These were the same halls she had hurried through years ago, her world consumed by exams, late-night study sessions, and—she hated to admit it—Jasper.

As they stepped into a small coffee shop just off the main quad, Cara let the warmth of the room thaw the chill in her bones. The place was exactly as she remembered it—wooden beams, the scent of espresso, the low hum of conversation. It was the kind of place that always seemed frozen in time, untouched by the years.

The line moved slowly, and Rachel was busy scrolling through her phone when Cara's ears caught a voice she hadn't heard in years and had hoped she'd never hear again.

"Yeah, it's just a quick trip. Dad wanted me to finalize the deal on the student housing project before Christmas."

Cara froze, her breath catching in her throat. She knew that voice—

smooth, polished, and faintly amused. She turned her head, and there he was. Jasper.

He stood a few feet away, his back turned to her as he spoke to someone at his table. He hadn't changed much. His dark hair was neatly styled, and his tailored coat screamed wealth and privilege. But it wasn't just him. Sitting beside him was a woman—a stunning blonde with an unmistakable air of sophistication. Her pregnancy was visible beneath her designer sweater, and her hand rested lightly on her belly as she listened to Jasper with a soft smile.

The light above their table caught a glint of gold, and Cara's stomach twisted as her gaze landed on the ring on the woman's finger. It was the same one Jasper had used to propose to her five years ago, his mother's original engagement ring before Victoria had upgraded to the three karat rock that had adorned her finger when Cara was still an honorary part of the Whitmore family.

"Cara?" Rachel's voice broke through her thoughts. She followed Cara's gaze, her expression tightening when she saw what Cara was looking at. "Oh, wow."

As if sensing their eyes on him, Jasper turned. For a brief moment, surprise flickered across his face, but it was quickly replaced by a charming smile—the same one Cara remembered all too well.

"Cara," he said smoothly, rising from his seat. "This is unexpected."

Jasper's charming smile widened as he stepped closer, his coat impeccably tailored, and his polished shoes clicking softly against the wooden floor. "Cara," he said again, more smoothly, his voice tinged with that familiar, practiced warmth. "Of all the places to run into you. It's been what—five years?"

Cara forced a polite smile, her hands tightening around her coffee cup. "Just over," she replied, keeping her tone neutral.

"You look... well," Jasper said, his eyes scanning her as though assessing a piece of furniture. "It's good to see you've found a way to keep busy."

Cara blinked, her stomach twisting. "I'm a lawyer," she said evenly. "I work in immigration law down in Texas."

Jasper arched a brow, his expression hovering between surprise and faint amusement. "Ah, of course. Always the humanitarian," he said with a slight chuckle, the edge in his tone almost imperceptible. "I imagine that must be... fulfilling. Though not exactly lucrative, I'd assume."

"It's not about the money," Cara replied sharply, her back straightening. "It's about helping people."

"Of course," Jasper said quickly, holding up a hand as if to placate her. "I didn't mean anything by it. It's admirable, really. You've always been... passionate."

Rachel, standing just behind Cara, narrowed her eyes but said nothing, letting the conversation play out as her gaze darted between the two of them.

"And what about you?" Cara asked, her voice cooler now. "Still working for your dad's company?"

Jasper's smile faltered slightly, but he recovered quickly. "Naturally," he said, slipping his hands into his pockets. "I'm overseeing some exciting developments—student housing near Lehigh, for one. Keeping the family legacy strong, you know."

Cara nodded, biting back the urge to respond with something bitter. It was the same Jasper—polished, confident, and just condescending enough to make her question herself.

There was a brief silence before Jasper's expression shifted, a little too practiced, as he gestured behind him. "Oh, where are my manners? Cara, Rachel, this is my wife, Jessica."

Cara's stomach sank as her gaze shifted to the tall, blonde woman who had risen from the table behind Jasper. Jessica was stunning—effortlessly elegant, her hair falling in perfect waves over the shoulders of her cream-coloured sweater. She extended a hand, her smile warm and polite. "It's nice to meet you," she said, her voice smooth, almost musical.

"Jessica," Jasper said, resting a hand lightly on her back, "this is Cara. We went to university together. And Rachel, of course," he added with a nod.

Cara forced herself to shake Jessica's hand, offering a tight smile. "Nice to meet you too," she managed, though the words felt heavy on her tongue.

Jessica rested a hand on her stomach, the soft curve of her pregnancy now unmistakable. "We're here for a quick trip before the holidays," she said lightly. "I wanted to see the campus Jasper always talks about. It's so beautiful."

"It is," Cara said softly, her eyes catching the glint of the ring on Jessica's finger again.

Jessica beamed, oblivious to the tension between the three of them. "We're expecting our first," she said, her hand brushing over her belly. "A little girl."

Jasper smiled, his hand moving to Jessica's shoulder. "She's due in March," he said, his tone smooth. "It's an exciting time for us."

Cara nodded stiffly, the weight of the moment pressing on her shoulders. She opened her mouth to say something, but Rachel stepped forward instead, her voice cool and cutting.

"Jessica," Rachel said, her eyes locking on the blonde woman. "If you ever need a way out, give me a call." Her tone was deceptively light, but the message was unmistakable.

Jessica's brow furrowed slightly, confusion flashing across her face, but she gave a polite smile. "Oh, that's kind of you. But I'm fine, really."

Rachel didn't respond, her gaze flicking to Jasper with a subtle sharpness that made him bristle. "I'm sure you are," she said dryly before turning back to Cara. "Ready to go?"

"Yeah," Cara said, her voice quieter now. She cast one last glance at Jessica, who was already turning back to Jasper, her perfect smile firmly in place.

As they stepped out into the cold, Cara let out a breath she hadn't realized she was holding. The air felt sharper, freer. Cara stood frozen for a moment, her thoughts racing. The familiar sting of his words lingered, each subtle barb a reminder of the years she had spent believing every cruel thing he'd ever implied about her. But this time, something was different. She wasn't the same person she had been five years ago.

It hadn't been easy.

After leaving Jasper, Cara had thought the worst was over. She'd told herself that the hardest part—the decision to walk away—was behind her. But she hadn't realized how much of herself she had lost in those four years with him, how much of her confidence and identity had been chipped away piece by piece.

The aftermath was brutal. Friends she had thought were hers turned away, choosing Jasper's charm and his version of the story over her painful truths. Whispers followed her, painting her as ungrateful, dramatic, and unstable. Her social circle, once wide and full of laughter, had shrunk to almost nothing. For months, it felt like she was swimming upstream, barely keeping her head above water.

Her parents were her anchor. They had wrapped her in unwavering support, their home becoming a refuge when the weight of it all threatened to crush her. Her mom, Martha, spent hours sitting with her at the kitchen table, offering gentle encouragement and reminding Cara of her worth. Her dad, Jim, rarely spoke about Jasper but always made a point to let Cara know how proud he was of her—just for making it through another day.

And Rachel—oh, Rachel. Cara hadn't expected her to stay. After everything Rachel had said, after the way she had sided with Jasper for so long, Cara had braced herself for her friend to disappear like so many others had. But Rachel had done the opposite. She had apologized, again and again, her voice breaking as she admitted how wrong she had been. "I should have seen it," she had said more times than Cara could count. "I should have been there for you."

At first, Cara hadn't known how to let Rachel back in. The betrayal had stung too much, the wounds too fresh. But Rachel had been relentless— not in pushing Cara to forgive her, but in showing up, in being there when Cara needed someone the most. Slowly, painfully, their friendship began to heal.

For Cara, healing came in small, uneven steps. Therapy became a lifeline —a space where she could unpack the years of manipulation and abuse, where she could begin to untangle the web Jasper had spun around her. Her therapist had helped her see the patterns, the ways Jasper had isolated and controlled her, and the lingering self-blame she carried. It was exhausting work, but little by little, she started to reclaim herself.

The decision to go to law school had been a turning point. She had chosen Texas, wanting to be far from the memories of Pennsylvania, and had been accepted to The University of Texas School of Law in Austin, one of the top programs in the country. The move had been terrifying, but also liberating —a chance to start fresh, to rebuild her life on her own terms.

She poured herself into her studies, finding purpose and strength in the work. Helping immigrants navigate the complexities of the legal system gave her a sense of fulfillment she hadn't thought possible. For the first time, she felt like she was truly making a difference.

But the scars didn't disappear overnight. There were nights when she lay awake, haunted by memories she couldn't shake. The way Jasper had twisted her words, the way his hands had lingered too long on her arms, leaving faint bruises she had convinced herself were nothing. The way he had made her feel small, over and over again, until she had started to believe it.

Yet, over time, those memories began to lose their grip. They didn't vanish completely, but they became smaller, less overwhelming. Cara learned to recognize her own strength—the strength it had taken to leave, to rebuild, to find herself again.

Now, standing on the steps of the same coffee shop she had frequented so many times as a student, Cara felt the crisp winter air sting her cheeks, but it wasn't unpleasant. It was grounding. Five years ago, this place had been her escape—somewhere to lose herself in the hum of caffeine-fueled conversations and the familiar rhythm of student life. Now, it was just a building, one that held memories but no longer had the power to define her.

She already knew she didn't need Jasper's validation. Cara had learned that hard truth long ago, in the moments of rebuilding her life. It had taken years of therapy, tears, and honest conversations with herself to let go of the part of her that still craved his approval. She had chosen herself, not for the first time today, but every single day since she had walked away from him. That choice wasn't always easy, but it was the one she had clung to, even when it felt like the world was trying to pull her back.

Cara exhaled, her breath visible in the cold air, and turned to Rachel, who was standing beside her. Rachel had been a constant—an anchor in Cara's healing. There had been a time when Cara had doubted their friendship could survive what had happened, but Rachel had proved her wrong. Her loyalty and unwavering support had become one of the brightest parts of Cara's life, a reminder that not everyone from her past had chosen Jasper over her.

"Are you okay?" Rachel asked softly, her eyes searching Cara's face.

Cara nodded, a small smile tugging at her lips. "Yeah," she said, and she truly meant it. "I think I am."

Rachel tilted her head, giving her a playful nudge. "You're more than okay. You're a badass lawyer who just had a front-row seat to her ex being the same smug jerk he always was. And you didn't let him get to you. That's growth."

Cara let out a soft laugh, the tension in her chest loosening. "I guess it is."

Rachel stepped closer, linking her arm with Cara's as they began walking back toward Rachel's car. "You've come so far, Cara. You should be proud of yourself. You've built this amazing life, and you're helping people every day. Meanwhile, Jasper is..." She trailed off with a shrug. "Well, let's just say Jessica might want to keep my number handy."

Cara shook her head, a real laugh escaping her this time. "You're terrible."

Rachel grinned. "No, I'm right. And you know it."

They walked in companionable silence for a moment, the snow crunching softly beneath their boots. Cara glanced up at the trees lining the path, their branches bare but dusted with frost. There was something beautiful about their starkness, their resilience. They stood tall and proud, even in the harshest of seasons. Cara felt a flicker of kinship with them, a strength she hadn't always known was hers.

"I'm proud of me too," she said finally, her voice quiet but firm.

Rachel gave her arm a squeeze. "Good. Because you deserve to be."

Cara smiled, her chest filling with something she hadn't felt in a long time

—peace. She wasn't defined by the past, by Jasper, or by the scars he had left behind. She was Cara Donovan, a lawyer, a fighter, a woman who had chosen herself. And that was more than enough.

The Woman She Became

A recent snowfall blanketed Jim Thorpe in insular white, the world around Cara was hushed and still. She stood on the back porch of her parents' house, her breath visible in the crisp winter air. The Audi she had once driven away from Lehigh had been replaced years before with a Chevrolet Trailblazer that now sat in her parents' driveway, dusted with snow. Her car was representative of who she truly was, not the version of herself that Jasper had tried to polish with his Midas touch.

It had been a few days since she'd run into Jasper Whitmore and his perfect, polished wife, Jessica. The encounter had lingered in her mind, not because of him, but because of how it had left her feeling—not broken, not small, but free. Seeing him with the same ring he had once offered her, with a life that was undoubtedly filled with the same hollow charm he had once used to control her, had only reinforced what she had known all along. Walking away had saved her.

For years, she had wondered if her choice to say no would haunt her forever, if it would leave her standing at the edge of her life, looking back with regret. But now, the answer she had given him felt like a gift—not to Jasper, but to herself. It was a declaration, a promise she had made to the girl who had stood trembling in her dorm room five years ago. She had chosen herself, not just once, but over and over again.

The screen door creaked open behind her, and Martha stepped out, a steaming mug of coffee in her hands. "Still thinking about it?" she asked, handing the mug to Cara and leaning on the porch railing beside her.

Cara shrugged, taking a sip. She had told her mom everything. In the wake of her relationship with Jasper, the two of them had become even closer.

"Not him," she said. "Not really."

"Then what?" Martha asked, her voice softer now.

Cara looked out at the snow-covered fields beyond her parents' yard. "How far I've come. How much further I want to go."

Martha smiled, nudging her shoulder. "You've already come so far, Cara. You should be proud."

"I am," Cara said, her voice steady. "But I think there's more."

Martha raised a brow. "Like what?"

Cara hesitated, the words forming in her mind like a song she hadn't heard in years but still knew by heart. "I want to keep fighting. For people who can't fight for themselves. For the ones who think their choices are already made for them." She exhaled slowly, her breath visible in the air. "I think that's what I was trying to do all along—prove to myself that we always have a choice."

Martha didn't say anything at first. She simply reached out, linking her arm with Cara's as they stared out at the horizon. "You know what I think?" she said finally, her tone playful but laced with sincerity.

"What?"

"I think you're going to change the world," Martha said, a grin tugging at her lips. "One case, one person, one impossible dream at a time."

Cara laughed softly, but the words settled over her like a promise. She hadn't changed the whole world, not yet, but she had changed her world. She had made the choice that mattered most, and everything else—the pain, the healing, the life she had built—had followed.

As the snow continued to fall, Cara set her coffee down on the railing and pulled her coat tighter around her. The cold didn't bother her much anymore. It had its own kind of clarity, a reminder of what it meant to stand firm, to weather the storm.

She turned to Martha, her voice quiet but unwavering. "Let's go back inside."

Martha nodded, following her as they stepped into the warmth of the house, leaving the cold behind them. Cara closed the door and paused, glancing back at the snow-covered world outside.

She had walked away from Jasper all those years ago, but more importantly, she had walked back to herself. And that, she knew now, was the answer she had always needed to give.

You've Reached The End But...
The Stories Never Stop

Songs To Stories is exactly what it sounds like—short, emotionally devastating, romantically charged, and occasionally unhinged novellas inspired by the one and only Taylor Swift. Because why simply listen to a song when you can spiral into an entire fictional universe about it?

A new novella drops on the 13th of every month, so if you have commitment issues, don't worry—you don't have to wait long for your next dose of heartbreak, longing, and characters making wildly questionable life choices in the name of love.

To keep up with the latest releases, visit BrittWolfe.com—or don't, and risk missing out while the rest of us are already crying over the next one. Your call.

See you at the next emotional wreckage.

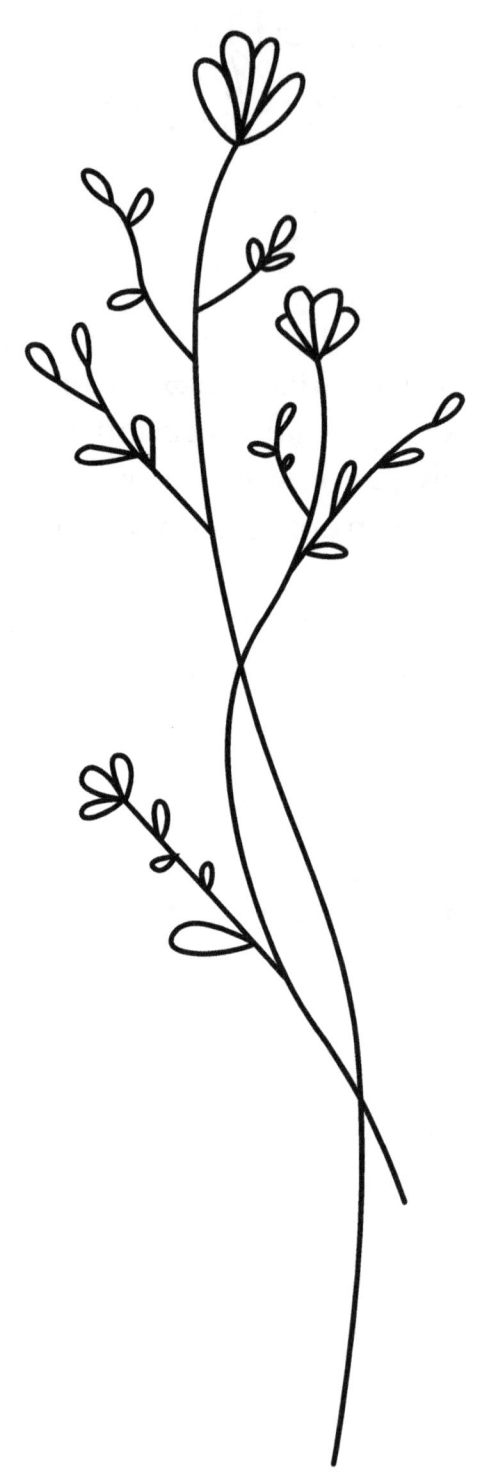

About The Author
Britt Wolfe

Britt Wolfe was born in Fort McMurray, Alberta, and now lives in Calgary, where she battles snow, writes stories, and cries over Taylor Swift lyrics like the proud elder Swiftie she is. She loves being part of a fan base that's as passionate as it is melodramatic.

She's married to a smoking hot Australian (her words, but also probably everyone else's), and together they parent two fur-babies: Sophie, the most perfect husky in the universe, and Lena, a mischievous cat who keeps them on their toes—and their furniture in shreds.

When Britt's not writing or re-listening to "All Too Well (10 Minute Version)," she's indulging her love for reading, potatoes in all forms, and the colour green. She's also a huge fan of polar bears, tigers, red pandas, otters, Nile crocodiles, and—because they're underrated—donkeys.

Her life is full of love, laughter, and just enough chaos to keep things interesting.

 @the.banality.of.britt

 BrittWolfe.com

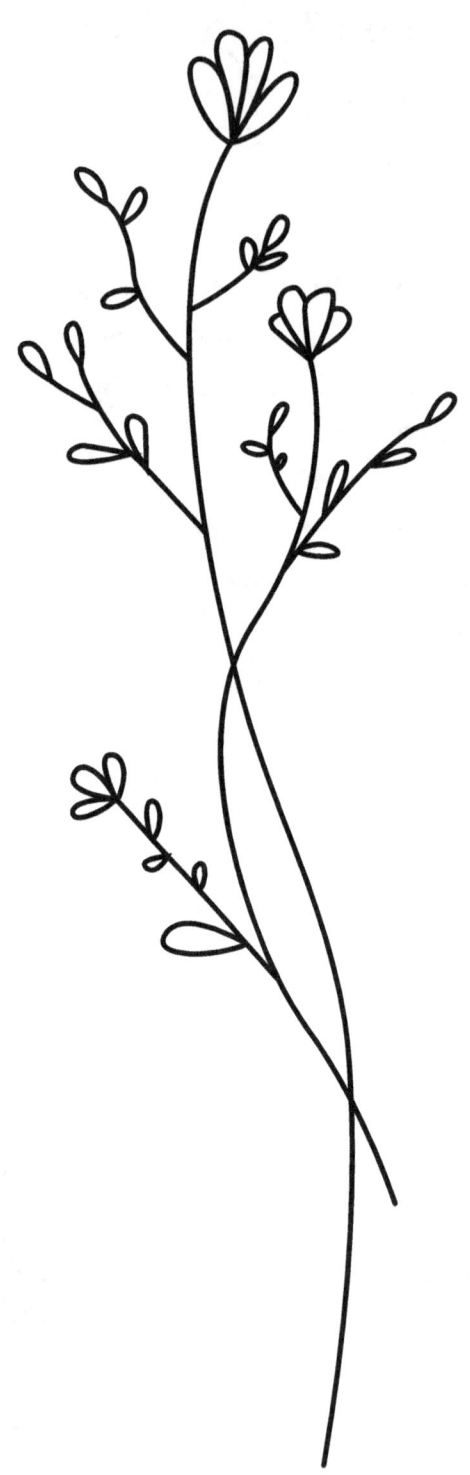

www.ingramcontent.com/pod-product-compliance
Lightning Source LLC
Chambersburg PA
CBHW082250120626
46555CB00009B/3028